Jacques & Spock

BY DAVID MICHAEL SLATER

ILLUSTRATED BY DEBBIE TILLEY

Clarion Books • New York

Clarion Books
a Houghton Mifflin Company imprint
215 Park Avenue South, New York, NY 10003
Text copyright © 2004 by David Michael Slater
Illustrations copyright © 2004 by Debbie Tilley

The illustrations were executed in Dr. Martin dyes and pen and ink on watercolor paper.
The text was set in 18-point Myriad Tilt.

www.houghtonmifflinbooks.com

Manufactured in China

Library of Congress Cataloging-in-Publication Data

Slater, David Michael.
Jacques and Spock / by David Slater ; illustrated by Debbie Tilley.
p. cm.
Summary: Jacques and Spock, two orange socks that are brothers, are
separated after Jacques is washed in the whites load of laundry.
ISBN 0-618-15980-0
[1. Socks—Fiction. 2. Brothers—Fiction. 3. Separation anxiety—Fiction.] I. Tilley, Debbie, ill. II. Title.
PZ7.S62898Jac 2004
[E]—dc22
2004000544

ISBN-13: 978-0-618-15980-2
ISBN-10: 0-618-15980-0

SCP 10 9 8 7 6 5 4 3 2 1

For Zach, Molly, Naava, Julia, Audrey,
Ryan, Ross, Emma, and especially MAX
—D.M.S.

For Dennis
—D.T.

"Right behind ya!" Jacques said, giggling. "Right in front of ya! Right behind ya! Right in front of ya!"

Spock wanted to joke with his brother, but soccer always made him nervous. He closed his eyes and held on as tightly as he could.

"Loosen up, Spock!" Jacques complained, but he knew it was no use.

The boy who wore Jacques and Spock was very unusual. All his possessions had to be orange, though he didn't take care of any of them. His clothes were always flung on the floor, and his toys were often broken or lost. His mini-basketball had been missing for months!

6

After soccer, the boy used Jacques and Spock for hoops practice. Spock held his breath in terror as he shot across the room. THUNK! He landed in the hamper. Jacques came flying right behind. "Above ya! Above ya! Look out below!" THUNK! He landed next to Spock, who was trembling.

Jacques sighed. Spock was scared of the dark. Comforting him in front of all the other laundry was embarrassing. "Humdey humdey hum hum," Jacques hummed as quietly as he could. Slowly, Spock began to settle down.

That afternoon, the brothers were taken to the laundry room. Only something went wrong. Spock went into the washer with the brights, as usual, but Jacques got mixed in with the whites!

Jacques wasn't worried. "Wheeeee!" he whooped, sloshing around in the soapy suds. For once he didn't have to worry about Spock getting sick during the spin cycle.

After he was dried, Jacques waited patiently on the counter.

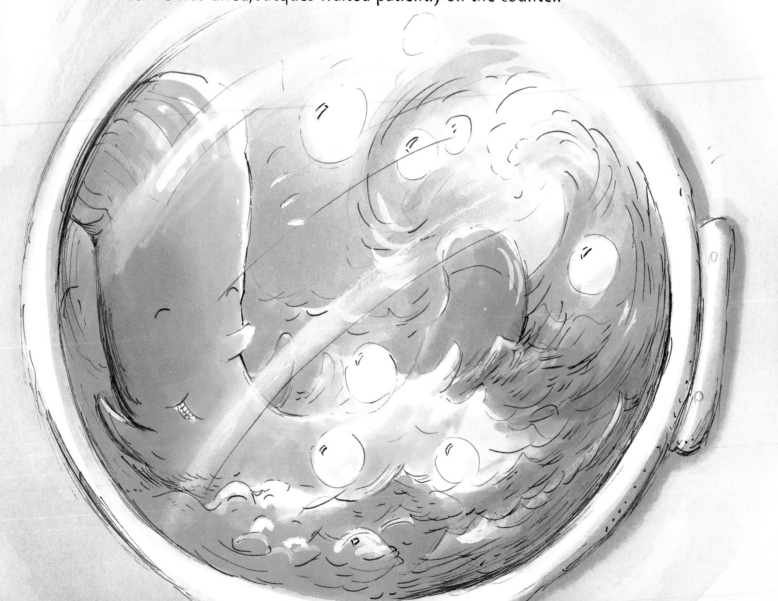

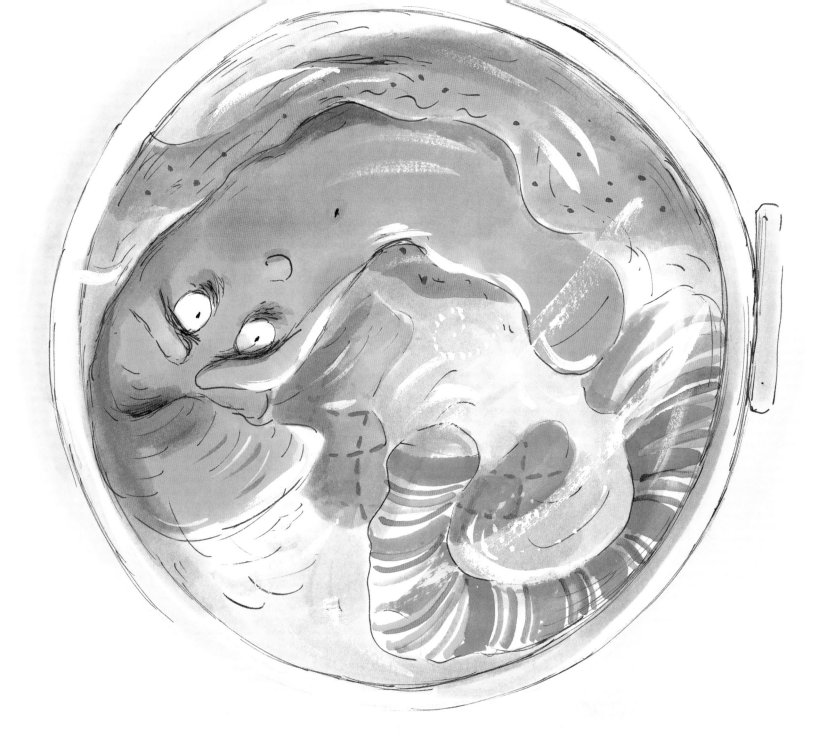

Getting laundered without his brother was an awful experience for Spock.
The washer made him dizzy, and the dryer was so hot he nearly fainted.

Then, when he finally saw Jacques, his eyes nearly popped out of their sockets. "You've . . . You've . . . You've . . . ," he sputtered, "You've . . . *changed colors!*" The dad had poured bleach into the washer to brighten the whites. Jacques was as white as a tube sock!

On the way back to the boy's room, Spock nearly came unraveled. "What will we do?" he whimpered. "The boy doesn't keep anything that's not orange!"

Jacques rolled his eyes. "Darn it, Spock!" he snapped. "Stop being such a hole in the heel!"

Spock lowered his head and didn't say anything more.

The next morning, the boy yanked Jacques out of the drawer. "IT'S NOT ORANGE!" he bellowed. "SOMEBODY RUINED MY SOCK!"

Spock tried with all his might to hold on to his brother, but he wasn't strong enough. "BE GONE!" shouted the boy as he hurled Jacques into the living room.

Jacques landed at the foot of the couch in a daze. *Tweee!* He thought he was hearing things. *Tweee!* He heard it again. Then he saw a small whistle blowing at him from under the couch. *"Psst! C'm'ere. Hurry!"* it whispered.

Jacques crawled under the couch and found himself surrounded by the boy's missing possessions. There were trading cards, stuffed animals, a hat with a propeller on top, and the mini-basketball!

"You're free, Sockman!" cried the hat. "I'd say this calls for a sock hop!" Everyone welcomed Jacques, and the dance party began.

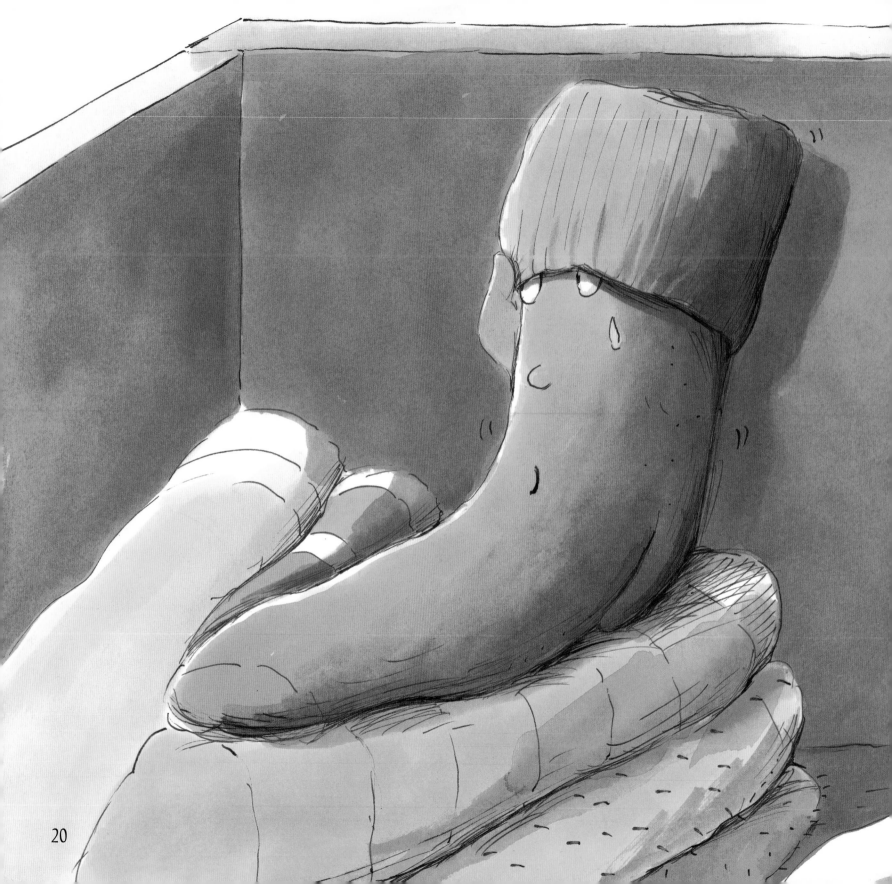

Spock lay drooped in his drawer all that day staring sadly toward the living room. "Oh, no! Oh, no!" he wailed. "What will I do without him?" He tried to soothe himself by humming, but he couldn't remember Jacques's tune. A lonely tear dripped down to the bottom of the drawer.

"It sure is a hard sock life," said a pair of underwear, trying to be supportive. It didn't help. Spock realized it was up to him to rescue his brother, but he just didn't know if he had the courage to try.

The sock hop under the couch went on for days. Jacques was having the time of his life not having to care for Spock, but after a while he began to worry. "What if Spock gets turned into a puppet?" he asked the propeller hat. "That's his greatest fear."

"Chill, Sockster," said the hat. "He'll be fine."

"I don't know," Jacques replied. "We've never been separated before. Spock can't stand to be more than a foot away from me."

"I used to miss my hoop," said the mini-basketball. "But life is better here. I'm sure your brother will get a new match soon enough, and then he'll forget all about you."

23

Jacques wasn't sure this was good news. He went to bed early that night and dreamed of Spock in the dark hamper searching for a sock to cling to for comfort. It was the first nightmare he had ever had, and it nearly made him weep. When he woke up, he realized something: a hole in the heel is far better than a hole in the heart.

A loud voice in the family room startled Jacques from his thoughts. "Young man," the father said sternly. "How many times have I told you not to leave your carrot juice on the coffee table? If it spills, it will leave a permanent stain."

When Jacques heard this, his eyes went wide with hope. Later on, he joined the dancing again. "Rock on, Sockmeister!" hooted the hat. "Sock it to us!" Jacques laughed, but he wasn't really having fun. He was only trying to make the day end faster.

That night, when everyone under the couch fell asleep, Jacques peeked into the family room. *The glass of juice was still there!*

Jacques looked at his snoozing friends. They were fun, but he couldn't let his brother down. He whispered goodbye and crept across the floor. Then he crawled up the leg of the coffee table and over to the glass. Carefully, he lowered himself into the juice and dunked himself under. He stayed curled up with his nose in the air for the rest of the night.

In the morning, the boy came in and picked up the glass. Jacques held his breath, hoping his plan had worked. Suddenly, he was pulled free. "WHO PUT MY SOCK IN A GLASS?" the boy hollered. *"ORANGE-O-RAMA!"*

The boy took Jacques back to his room, balled him up, and tossed him into the hamper, where he landed on something soft and shaking. It was Spock.

"Jacques? Is that you?" Spock asked when he dared to open his eyes. He saw that it was. "I tried to rescue you!" he cried. "I really, really tried! Only, the mom found me on the floor and threw me in here, and then I was too scared to climb back out. Will you ever forgive me, Jacques? Will you?"

"Don't sweat it, Spock," Jacques said. "I'm sorry, too. Would you like me to hum to you?"

"Well," Spock replied, "maybe if you hum *with* me, someday I'll be able to do it for myself."

"I'm right with ya," said Jacques.

"I'm right with ya, too," said Spock.

Jacques and Spock smiled at each other. "Humdey humdey hum hum," they hummed … as loudly as they could.